Mrs. Adams

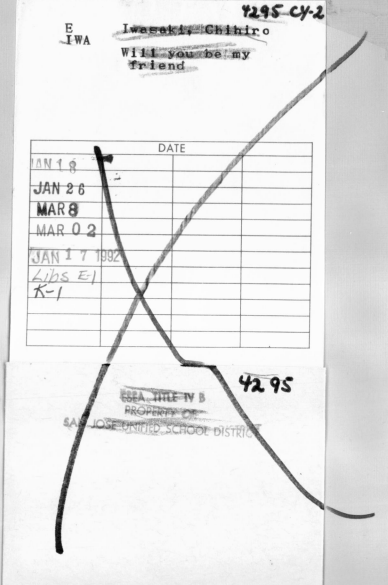

4295 CY-2

E
IWA

Iwasaki, Chihiro

Will you be my friend

DATE		
JAN 1 8		
JAN 2 6		
MAR 8		
MAR 0 2		
JAN 1 7 1992		
Libs E-1		
K-1		

42 95

© THE BAKER & TAYLOR CO.

Will You Be My Friend

by Chihiro Iwasaki

McGRAW-HILL BOOK COMPANY
New York St. Louis San Francisco

Cataloging in Publication Data appears on last page.

One bright, sunny morning, Allison was playing in front
of her house when she saw a truck loaded with furniture
drive slowly down the street.

"Please stop next door," Allison said. She crossed
her fingers. There was a loud crashing "bang," and
the truck stopped. Allison crawled under the hedge, her
favorite hideout. Hours seemed to creep by while she
played with her paints and watched the moving men
unload the truck. At last Allison saw a bicycle.

There must be *someone* for me to play with, she thought.

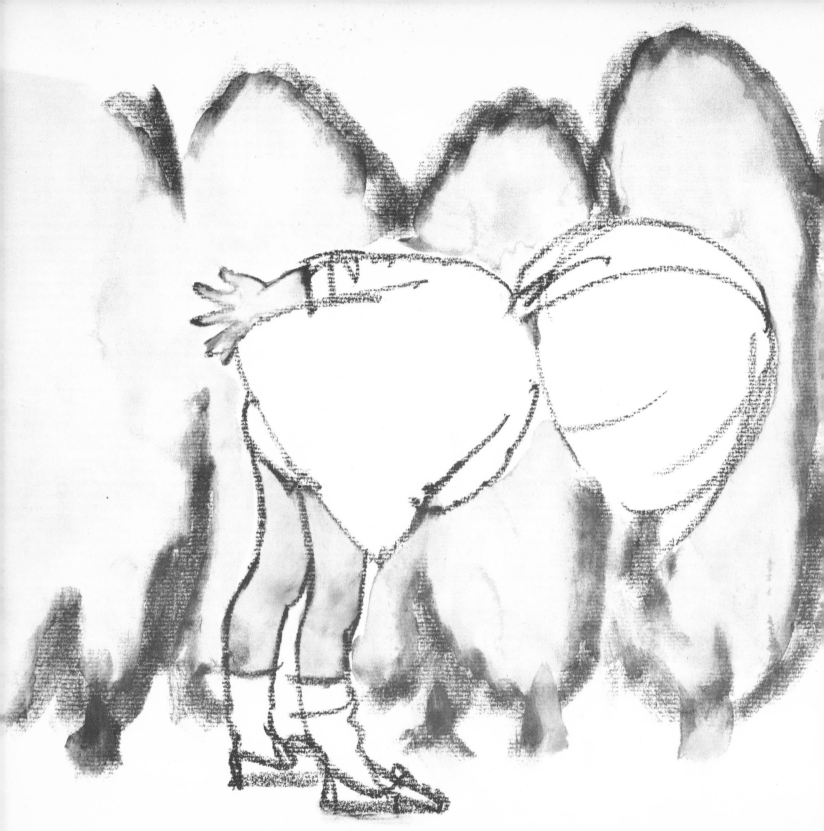

Just then Allison heard someone

in the yard next door.

It was a boy. Allison knew just what she wanted to say to him, "Will you be my friend?"

But before she got a chance to say a word, the boy turned and walked away.
"O.K. boy," Allison shouted, "I don't care."

The boy raced around the yard. Then he climbed up
a tree, and started to swing from a branch.
"Humphf—anybody can do that," Allison muttered.
"I know what I'll do."

Allison went into her house.
A few minutes later she came out again,
dressed in her mother's favorite shawl
and high-heel shoes. She even carried
her mother's prettiest purse.

That afternoon
Allison and her dog Tippy were playing.
The boy came out of his house and
started to walk his dog. But the dog
was so big, it broke away from him
and chased poor Tippy out of the yard.

Allison looked out of her window
before she went to bed that night.
The big dog was still chasing Tippy.

"That boy is trouble," Allison said.
"What am I going to do?"

In the morning, Allison asked her mother whether she might
eat her cornflakes and milk outdoors.

The boy was there already.
He was drinking milk, too.

Suddenly,
he went over to Allison
and growled,

"I'm a monster!"
Allison giggled.
"Oh, what fun!
I'll be a ghost."

She ran over to the clothesline and took a sheet that was drying off the line. But she was too excited to notice a big puddle underneath. She tripped and down she fell!
Poor Allison was so embarassed. She ran and hid under the hedge.

"What's the matter with her?" Allison heard
the boy ask his mother.

He'll never want to be my friend now, Allison thought. Well, I'm not going to bother with him anyway. He's trouble!

She was leaning up against the hedge, moping,
when she heard the boy call,
"Hey, girl. What's your name? I'm Mike.
What have you got there under the hedge?
What would *you* like to play? Will you
be my friend?"

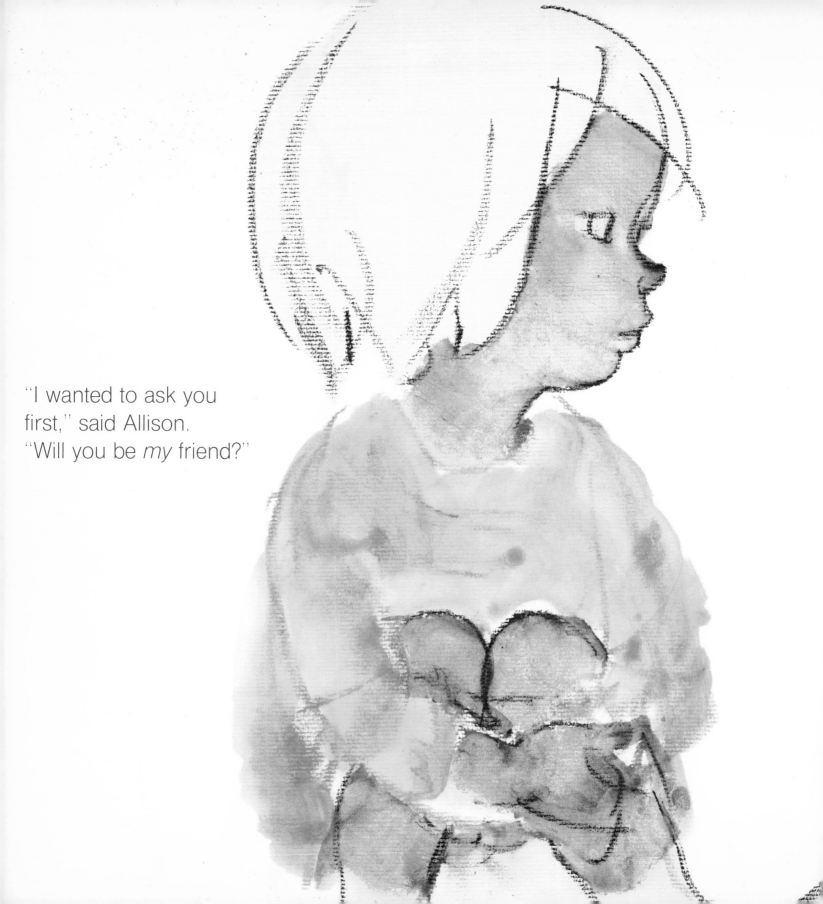

"I wanted to ask you
first," said Allison.
"Will you be *my* friend?"

"Oh—that's all right,"
Mike said. "Would you
like to play with
my new tennis ball?"

"I would like to very much," said Allison. "But first—
and she ducked under the hedge and brought out her paint box
—"let's play with my paints. My name is Allison."